This edition first published in 2001
by Cat's Whiskers
96 Leonard Street, London EC2A 4XD

Cat's Whiskers Australia
56 O'Riordan Street, Alexandria NSW 2015

ISBN 1 903012 28 7

0 Hachette Livre 2000
English text 0 Cat's Whiskers 2001

A CIP catalogue record for this book is
available from the British Library

Printed in France : Pollina S.A., 85400 Luçon-N

ANNE GUTMAN · GEORG HALLENSLEBEN

George is Jealous

CAT'S Whiskers

THE WATTS PUBLISHING GROUP LTD

It was Lily's birthday.
My birthday was in a week's time,
but I was already bigger than Lily.
My mother bought me a present to give her.

At the party, everyone had brought
presents for Lily. Some people had even
given her the same present.
She got lots of silly girly things;

and then Lily opened her last present, the one
her parents had given her. She'd kept it to the end.
She already **knew** what it was, though!
I couldn't believe my eyes ...

... there were the in-line skates, the **brilliant** ones
with a red flash and special wheels to go up stairs,
my skates, that I'd been talking about for
over a month! What's more, she'd got all the gear
that went with them, even the anti-mist goggles.

Luckily, to please her grandmother,
Lily had to try on her new
ballet shoes, and while she was
doing that ...

... I took the skates and
quickly hid them in my bag.

Everything was fine until Lily wanted to
try on her skates. **DISASTER!**
They'd disappeared. Everyone panicked and
started to look for them. Lily started to cry.

I pretended to look for
the skates under the bed.

I stayed there a long time.
Nobody seemed to notice. They were all
far too busy comforting Lily.

At school, it was just the same,
they only had time for Lily.
All anybody was interested in was
the mystery of Lily's skates.

Even on my birthday, she was **still** going on about them. And then, when I opened my present, she started to cry again ...

I did lots of amazing tricks on my skates!
But Lily wouldn't talk to me any more. She said
that seeing me made her feel even more unhappy.

In the end, I got rather bored
skating on my own all the time.
So, one day, very quietly ...

... I returned her skates.

Lily could never quite work out how
they'd got on top of the cupboard.
But since then, every day ...

... I'm much faster than she is!